One Man's Grief
and a
Long Walk

One Man's Grief
and a
Long Walk

James A W Schmidt

Charleston, SC
www.PalmettoPublishing.com

One Man's Grief and A Long Walk

Copyright © 2021 by James A W Schmidt

All rights reserved.

First Edition

Paperback ISBN: 978-1-63837-723-8
eBook ISBN: 978-1-63837-724-5

I dedicate this book to my late wife, Patricia.
She showed me what real love, faith, courage,
and strength was all about.

(1952-2009)

Table of Contents

ACKNOWLEDGMENTS

To the late Bill Russell who introduced me to the joy of writing and his writer's group that he founded.

To the James River Writers Group in Huron SD, who critiqued my chapters and helped me tighten my sentence structure and made me dig deeper into my emotions.

To Brian Schmidt who without him the hike would not have happened.

To Tim and Gayle Tescher for opening their home to us and driving us to the trail. We couldn't have done it without them.

To Duane who stood by me at my time of grief and watched over Rufus and Rosey as I was on the trail.

To the grief support group whom gave me the tools to help me heal.

To a supportive family who didn't think I was nuts.

CHAPTER ONE

This journey began in a deep dark hole. One so deep I couldn't see the light looking up. It wasn't a literal hole, but an emotional one that held me down. I felt so isolated, so alone.

The present felt unbearable. Happiness was in the past. I just couldn't see my future. What brought me to this emotional pit? Grief. On November 2, 2009, I lost my beloved wife, Patricia, to cancer. After 36 years and two kids she was gone. To make things worse, I lost my job a short time later.

Patricia was my world. We did everything together. She would roll up her sleeves and tackle anything. We worked hard to put food on the table, but we did it together. Both of us had two jobs. She was a school lunch lady and refinished furniture after work. I was a maintenance man by day, and after supper, I helped with stripping, sanding, and finishing chairs, tables, and any other task that was in front of me. We worked together until about 11:00 p.m. and then went to bed just to do it all over again the next day. Even with all the time spent working, we never lost sight of why we did it. Patricia and I felt like the kids needed to enjoy life, not just see their parents working all the time. Family was important to us. We would find ways to go camping or go on vacations. Those days were so different from now.

With all this time on my hands, I was left to my thoughts. If only this pain could go away. I could see how someone could die of a broken heart. My thoughts began to scare me. Did I have a reason to live? As if to answer my own question, thoughts of my daughter, Christy, and her husband, Jonathon, came to mind, and my grandkids. Next my son Brian came to mind. Christy and Brian had lost their mother. If I hadn't snapped out of this emotional pit they may have lost their dad too. Life had to have purpose, a goal, something to look forward to.

Patricia used to have a strange ability to dream about the future. I was a skeptic. A number of times I brushed off her prophetic messages until they came to pass. Her foretold dreams always seemed to be something tragic. Those mornings after she'd had one of those dreams, I would find her sitting up in bed and waiting for me to wake up so she could share it. I came to recognize the signs, and I would brace myself. To me this was not a gift; it was more like a curse.

One morning I woke up to her just sitting there. She sat there not saying anything. That morning she was slow to share and it put me on edge. I sat up beside her and listened intently as she began to inform me of her dream.

She began, "I stood before a long tunnel and knew I had to go through. There was no other choice. Inside, it was very dark. A narrow walkway went right down the middle. A violent stormy sea raged on both sides of the path with waves that showed no mercy to those who fell in. I focused on the pathway before me. After a long time of stumbling in the darkness, I saw a tiny light up ahead. Step by step, I moved toward it. With each step the exit got brighter and brighter. When I finally got to the end of the tunnel, I saw the Lord in a brilliant white robe with arms open and calling to me. As I reached Him, He wrapped His arms around me and said, 'I love you.'

"Jim, please listen carefully, I think I'm going to have a hard road ahead of me, and we might not get to grow old together."

I was at a loss for words, so we just hugged each other tight.

The day we got the news about her cancer, it hit me like a ton of bricks, but to Patricia, it came as no surprise. She promised to fight it for the family's sake, and she gave it her best shot.

When she was close to the final journey, she made me promise that I would get better and heal in time. Shortly after that she peacefully went into the arms of the Lord.

I guess the best way to honor her memory would be to keep my promise. But nothing felt like life would ever get better. How did other people survive this pain and loneliness? To seek help just wasn't natural for a guy, at least not for me. I guess it was pride. A man has to have his pride, you know. I've never seen any medals handed out to the man with the most stubborn pride, but he sure hangs on to it like it is worth something. The Bible says pride comes before a fall. I didn't feel like I could fall any farther.

I felt like a bug in a mason jar trying to get out. Each time I tried, I just slipped back down. The attempt seemed useless. I began to think that maybe I should just roll over on my back and die.

One day as I sat in my easy chair watching an old rerun a pain hit my chest. My arm felt numb and my breathing labored. But instead of calling 911, I sat back and smiled. Okay, Lord take me home. Patricia is waiting for me. To my disappointment the pain subsided. My doctor said it was just an anxiety attack.

Loneliness settled in like arthritis to every part of my body. Depression was an invisible partner that taunted me about my pain. I cried out *"How do I stop all this?"* Then that quiet voice within said, *you know the answer. You made a promise, remember?"* With that thought, I completely broke down and sobbed bitterly until I was exhausted.

Most nights were hard for me, but somehow I got a better night's sleep after the breakdown. The next morning felt different. It was time to roll up my sleeves and go to work. First, I kicked my pride out the backdoor. Looking for a grief support group was top of the list. After finding one, I wrote down the time and place. Because I made a promise, there was no backing out. *I can do this!*

CHAPTER TWO

I couldn't move, sitting in the parking lot. Staring at the entry way, my feet felt glued to the floorboard and my hands gripped the steering wheel so hard my knuckles were turning white. *I can't do this* I told myself. There was still time to back out of this grief support meeting. A low gruff voice from within said, *"You have to do this, you made a promise.* "I don't want to be here!" I replied as I pounded my fist on the steering wheel. Looking around I wondered if anyone had seen or heard me. They probably would have thought I was nuts. Maybe I was. *"You're a coward!* "Sometimes that inner voice can be so loud that it comes out verbally.

A shuffling sound broke my train of thought. An elderly lady with a walker slowly moved through the light powder of early January snow toward the church doors. My face slowly dropped. I'm a Vietnam vet and this lady put me to shame.

Slowly I got out of the car and headed to the door. Inside I was greeted by a lady with a pleasant smile. "Hello, I'm Deb.

Welcome to our grief support group. Just head down the hall and turn right to room 101."

Turning the corner I saw a small table with empty name tags and some markers. Putting on the tag, my legs felt weak as I reluctantly walked to the door. My heart pounded as I entered the room. There was a large table with about a dozen chairs around it. Most were already occupied. I felt as though all eyes were on me as I stepped into the room. It was tempting to turn and run, but I had gotten this far so I ambled to the closest empty chair and sat down. The room was mostly filled with women. There was only one other guy besides me. My biggest fear was that they would call on me to say something. I squirmed in my seat and my right foot started to nervously bounce up and down. The only way to stop it was to put my hand on my knee. Then the left foot started up so I had my hands on both knees.

At the head of the table, a different lady stood up and introduced herself. "Hello I'm Jane and I will be your facilitator or group leader. Congratulations, you have just accomplished one of the hardest things you could do—a walk through that door for the first time." Then she introduced us to members of her team." Let's go around the table and introduce ourselves, then share our loss. Remember, if you're not ready to share just say pass. I'll start. I'm Jane and I lost my husband five years ago to cancer."

As we went around the table, I kept telling myself, I can do this. When it was my turn, I took a deep breath and said, "Hey, I'm Jim and I lost my wife on November 2nd to cancer. I sighed. I'm doing this.

After the introductions, Jane shared a few rules of confidentiality to help us all feel safe.

"Now let's take a break. The restrooms are down the hall to the right. We have some coffee and treats for you, enjoy."

My ears perked up when I heard coffee. Oh coffee my old friend. It's like an inner hug with each sip.

During break, I caught up with Jane. "I see you only have two of us guys here, is it usually that way?"

"Unfortunately, that's the case. For generations men have been taught from childhood to grow up, big boys don't cry, don't be a crybaby. They have been conditioned to keep all their feelings inside. That advice is the worst advice you can give to anyone. It sabotages a person's emotional wellbeing. I wish there was someone who could encourage more men to come. "

We returned to our seats for the rest of the meeting. I put on my fake smile; if they only knew how I felt inside, they might move further away from me.

As others began to share, I was surprised to hear that I was not alone in my feelings and emotions. With the focus on myself, it just didn't occur to me that others felt that out-of-control feeling and intense pain. I began to feel a kindred spirit with this group. It no longer was just all about me. A lump began to form in my throat as I realized this room was full of hurting people. Can we help each other through this dark journey? Maybe I can fit in here. More of my knotted up tension throughout my body vaporized. A weird compulsion to speak came over me. But what if it comes out sounding stupid? Would anyone understand? With a deep breath I began. "I just can't bring myself to remove her toothbrush from its holder."

Bracing myself for a long awkward silence. I waited.

Jane responded, "That's not uncommon when it comes to a loved one's things. Has anyone else struggled with something like this?"

Then someone sniffed and said, "Yaw, me too, my husband's toothbrush is still there also." She then reached for a tissue.

A number of heads nodded in agreement. We began to talk about our loved one's clothing.

Betty, the lady with the walker, spoke up, "My kids want me just to get rid of George's clothing. I don't feel ready to do that yet."

"Talk to your kids, let them know how you feel, and tell them when you are ready to deal with it, then they can help. That's my suggestion." Jane replied.

"I'll get them together sometime this week," Betty responded.

It was suggested that only when we were ready did we have to deal with that. It could take a year or two. There was nothing wrong with keeping some things, but to keep everything was not healthy.

I didn't like opening up to strangers, but these people didn't feel like strangers. We all had one thing in common, our loss and pain. I felt safe there. After clearing my throat, I began:

"All my life I tried to avoid getting hurt. I stayed away from bullies. In the service I kept my head down, but I couldn't avoid this one. It hurts just to talk about it."

Because of a lump in my throat, I couldn't continue.

"Jim, none of us can avoid or run from grief, Jane responded, we don't get over it, we have to get through it."

That advice stuck with me.

As I left the room that night, I had a lot to ponder in my thought process. It was a relief to know my actions were normal, that made me feel better. The group gave me some tools to deal with my pain. I knew the journey of grief was a long one, but I have a place to turn to. I'm was not alone.

CHAPTER THREE

With each group meeting I attended, I learned a lot about myself and gained some helpful coping skills.

In one meeting we discussed our identities. There are labels we place on ourselves. I can say I am depressed, or I can't do something because I am depressed. Therefore that is who I am, a depressed person. A video in class suggested this. I am a father, someone's son, and I am dealing with depression. Depression is not who we are, it's what we are going through.

It's strange how our identity can change in a flash.

I felt like my identity was ripped away the day I lost my wife. I was no longer a husband--a part of a couple.

When discussion time came around, I shared something that happened to me as I was applying for an ID card at the veteran's administration.

"A gentleman was helping me fill out the paperwork and asked me a number of questions. When it came to marital status, I said single. But in further discussion he found out I lost my wife, he went back and crossed out single and circled widower.

I felt my body tense up and my face got warm. It took a lot of self-control to not lash out at him. I hated that title. I didn't ask for it. Ripping into him wouldn't change the facts, so I let it go. "It seemed that by the nodding of heads around the table, the group understood. Others shared similar stories. One thing we all agreed on was lashing out at someone doesn't help, and changes nothing.

Each meeting we covered different hurdles we might face on our grief journeys. One of my biggest hurdles was facing the future. To move forward I must first look ahead. That seemed so simple, but when it came to grief, looking ahead was far from simple. In fact, anxiety was what I felt for the future. I kept waiting for the other shoe to drop. After what I'd been through, can anything good ever happen to me again? As we were discussing the subject of the future it made me squirm in my chair. Yet I knew that unless I faced the future I could not move forward in my journey of grief.

I needed a reason to look ahead, some kind of purpose. If I had no purpose, it would be easy to give up. Setting goals was a good way to find purpose. I drew a blank when it came to future plans and goals. There was only one goal I had at the time--that was to get through the intense pain of grief. I needed to heal.

Before I could face anything, I needed to figure out where my sources of strength would could from. It didn't take long to come up with some.

There were three sources that could help me through hard times; I called them my three F's. They were, Faith, Family, and Friendship.

My faith has gotten me through numerous struggles in life, but this hurdle was huge. I thought I had a strong faith, but this loss really tested it. It hurt like hell to have God take Patricia away from me like that. Yes, I was mad at God. I knew God knew my heart, and as I prayed to Him, I was honest to share how I felt. Faith is a powerful thing. I couldn't imagine going through this without it.

There were Bible verses that gave me some comfort also. It showed me that God really did care what happened to me. The Psalms have a lot of comforting verses, like this one.

God is our refuge and strength
an ever-present help in trouble.
Psalms 46:1

Family support was a key element. My mom and siblings were there for me. Coming from a family of five kids, I remember the conversations around the supper table. It was a household rule that we all ate together. Table talk ranged from daily achievements to struggles we had. Sometimes disagreements were settled at the table. That open conversation carried into our adult lives. During those times of intense grief, long talks on the phone with my family helped get me through hard spells.

We used to only hug on special occasions, like if we would go away for a while, but after Patricia's passing, good- by hugs became common. Hugs brought us even closer than before. I know that when there are pandemics, we need to take precautions. It's nice to know there are warnings if there are any strains around. When we get an all clear I'm a hugger.

When it comes to family, sometimes we need to mend fences because I found that offence and defense are fine in football, but not in family arguments, being right can be overrated. When I wave the white flag in surrender, over some petty argument, we all win. Close family ties bring strong support. There is a lot of peace and freedom in reconciliation. With bigger battles, I look for God's help as we work to find common ground.

I had learned a few things about friendship through my loss. There were acquaintances, people I knew, and closer friends, the people I shared things with and did things with. Couples got together with couples. The loss of a spouse can test friendships. Things changed when Patricia went to Glory. People felt awkward around me and some treated me like a disease, like they could lose a loved one by just hanging around me. It hurt when old friends would try not to make eye contact as we passed on the street. Some people might duck into a store or change course if they saw me. I knew it was hard to know what to say. "Hi Jim, how's it going?" probably wasn't the best greeting. Maybe something like," it's a good day for a walk." I didn't care if they stumbled on their words, at least they tried. I was lonely for conversation.

Part of my new normal was making new friends. There were days I just had to get out of the house. I would wander around the mall and shopping centers just to be around people. On one occasion, I ran into Duane. It had been a while since we had seen each other. We must have talked for half an hour or more. At one point I asked Duane if he would like to go for coffee once a week since we enjoyed visiting so much we set up a day and time. He's now become my best friend.

Knowing I had all this support from my faith, family, and friends, really helped me move forward. I wasn't so alone.

The world was so different to me, it was hard adjusting. In the past Patricia and I made decisions together. Now it's all on me. Cooking was trial and error and eating out alone felt weird. I got to be quite the chief at hotdogs and TV dinners. After a while, I got use to dining out by myself. Sometimes I'd be invited to sit at someone's table. That was a good way to show they cared.

But with this new normal came opportunity. I could recreate myself. This was where planning came in. Having my mind on creative opportunities helped me not to focus on my loss. Sometimes it was hard to stay on task but having a project sure could help.

What kind of things did I like to do? I already belonged to an oil painting group. It was therapeutic, so I stayed with it. My paintings came from photos I took along the way, so I joined a photo club to improve my subject material.

One day something unexpected came along. Bill Russell was the founder of a local writers group. He invited me to join him at a meeting. Having dyslexia made reading more difficult for me, so I was skeptical. How could I write if I was a slow reader? But when I got into it, it was a blast! With each group, I made new friends, and new adventure came my way. I was already journaling in the grief support group, so why not try something new. Poetry and short stories was my thing.

Knowing where my support came from did help and the different groups and hobbies lifted me up somewhat, but I needed a bigger, more challenging goal to look forward to. At one time, I ran 5ks, but had never run a marathon. It would have taken a lot of conditioning to prepare. All that to run for four to six hours, then it would be over.

A trip to Europe would have been great, but that was beyond my pocketbook. I needed an adventure. Some place I'd never been before. Just the thought of it gave me a rush.

As a boy on the farm, I walked every square foot of the place, with dreams of being an explorer. There was always the desire to hike a famous trail, to see what was around the next bend. I was still in pretty good shape physically. It seemed I was too busy to dream about exploring. To go off on some adventure just wasn't possible. Could this be the time to go exploring? Sure! Why not go for it! Suddenly, I was filled with anticipation! I felt alive again. It had been some time since I felt like this. Wow, to dream of adventure again. Just thinking of walking somewhere, I've never explored before, brought the kid back in me. This goal was possible. In fact it was doable.

CHAPTER FOUR

Even though I dreamed of some kind of adventure, my journey of grief was like a roller coaster ride. Sometimes things were bearable, but sometimes it was the pits. Night time was really hard. As the sun went down in the west, so would my mood. The nights were so lonely. The bed was so cold and empty. I missed those bed time talks. Hugging a pillow brought me little comfort. My heart ached for her presence.

If it weren't for Rufus and Rosey, my two Welsh Corgis, I would have gone crazy. They were my emotional support dogs. Their personalities were so different. Rosey was more verbal, she let me know when it was time to go out. She spoke for both of them. When Rufus needed out, he got Rosey worked up to where she thought it was her idea. Rufus loved to play. He was like a puppy. The dog toys were his, she cared less. Rosey was a no nonsense girl. Rufus and I liked tug-of-war. But that game was beneath her dignity.

When I was down and depressed, it was Rosey who came up to me first to comfort me, then Rufus would follow. Just scratching their ears and petting them, made me feel a little better. They would look up at me with eyes that seemed to say, "We miss her too, but you still have us." Doctors say that petting an animal is great therapy. Many hospitals and nursing homes have therapy dogs. I thanked God for them.

Rosey was content to sleep in her little bed, but Rufus would sneak up on the bed from time to time. Patricia hadn't liked dogs on the bed. After she was gone, I needed his company. So when Rufus jumped up on the bed, there was no commanding him to get down. The feeling of warmth and movement brought me comfort. With Rufus by my side, the bed didn't seem so cold and lonely.

Rufus and I would play this game where I would throw the covers over him and roll him around. He would go R-R-R-R-R till I pulled the covers off, then he'd look at me to do it again. When he got tired of it, we would lie back to back and go to sleep. Those dogs really helped me though some hard times. They were there for me.

I woke up thinking about my goals. A goal would only be a dream if I only thought about it, and took no action. It was time to do the research. Ever since I was a boy, I always wanted to explore. The desire to walk a famous trail picked up my spirits. One of the best was right here in South Dakota, the George Mickelson Trail. After getting on my computer and checking out some facts about the trail, I ordered an information packet from the South Dakota Department of Tourism. It wasn't very long and this big envelope came in the mail packed with all kinds of good stuff, even discounts on things in the Black Hills area. Just physically spreading the maps, pamphlets, and information on the table energized me. My pulse quickened. I was like a little boy on Christmas morning.

The maps of the trail showed all the trail heads, toilets, water stations, and elevations along the way. With all the pamphlets, I got lost in the photos. This trail winds through the beautiful Black Hills. There were four tunnels along the way. I couldn't wait to walk though those tunnels. The trail also has about a 100 bridges. It starts in Edgemont and goes 109 miles to wind up in Deadwood. Hiking over a 100 miles wouldn't be easy. Careful planning was required to make this hike safe and enjoyable.

I picked up a pamphlet on the history of the Mickelson Trail. As I thumbed through it, I found the history fascinating.

Back in the 1890s, gold was discovered in the Black Hills, and the rush was on. People from all over flocked to this place to strike it rich. Mining companies began to spring up to dig up more ore for more gold. The biggest gold mine in the hills was the Homestake Mine by Deadwood-Lead. The Burlington Northern Railroad ran supplies to the mine for many years. The tracks carved their way across the entire hills from the north to the south.

In 1929, a short, little guy named John Perret, while panning for gold along Potato Creek found the biggest gold nugget ever found in the hills. It was 7 3/4oz. He instantly became the biggest man in Deadwood. From that time on the locals called him Potato Creek Johnny. Travelers would look him up just to hear his stories of adventure. There is an example of the nugget at the Adams Museum down town.

When the Homestake Gold Mine closed, there was no need for the railroad, so it was abandoned.

Sometime, in the 1980s, around a 100 years after the rails began, a plan came up to convert the old abandoned railroad line into a biking trail. A solid base and many bridges were already in place. With the tunnels, it made it the perfect trail. When George Mickelson became governor, he pushed for work and funding for the trail. The wheels of the project began to move. It was full steam ahead.

Unfortunately, Governor Mickelson never got the chance to see it completed.

I remember turning on the TV to watch the local news one day in 1993. The camera was panning across a massive fire, and then it came to a big plane tail. What on earth? Turning up the volume, I could hardly believe what I was hearing. The news sent a shockwave all across the state. That day South Dakota lost its governor and his crew in a terrible plane crash.

In 1998, the Black Hills trail was completed. The base was made of packed crushed limestone and gravel, perfect for a bike trial. The bridges were repaired and renovated to fit a new purpose. The tunnels were shored up and made safe. In honor of our late former governor, the trail was named the George S. Mickelson Trail.

It's been a little while since I called Christy, my daughter. I'm sure she would have liked to know what I had in mind. She reminds me of her mother. Christy is full of energy and ready to take on the world. When it comes to projects, she likes to roll up her sleeves and go-for- it. To see that energy in Christy makes me feel that not everything is lost.

Her response to my plans was not, Dad, are you nuts? She just simply said "Wow! That's great; it sounds like the adventure of a lifetime."

The more I read about the trail the more I was riveted to it. All the ratings were positive. I could picture walking along hearing the birds singing and the smell of the pine trees. It all sounded like heaven on earth.

CHAPTER FIVE

When I made plans, I liked using the bulletin board method. Here is an example:

WHAT - Yard Sale

WHERE - Location

WHEN – May 19th

I'm sure you get the idea. So with the Mickelson Trail it was like this:

WHAT- Mickelson Trail

WHERE- Black Hills

WHEN- To be determined

The best time to hike the hills was summer; June can still be a little cool at night. Winter was totally out of the question because I hated the cold. As a maintenance man, it was my job to do the snow removal. All I had was a mower with a snow thrower mounted on it. There was no cab so I got covered with snow in the subzero weather. I had to have things cleared out before the first employees came to work.

July or August looked favorable. July was the height of tourist season, and the first week of August was the Sturgis Motorcycle Rally. In mid-August the hills started to quiet down, so this felt like the best time to hike the trail. Okay, I could mark off the WHEN.

As a 60 year old guy, it probably wasn't a good idea to walk it alone. Who could I get to go with me on this great adventure? I didn't want a stranger for this trip, and it had to be someone in as good a shape or better than myself.

Looking at a trail map, I saw that the trail was a little more than 100 miles. Whoever I picked to walk with me had to move at a pace that could cover more than 25 miles in one day. It would take some conditioning to brisk- walk long distances. If I added up hill climbs, and short rest stops, the physical strain could be challenging. We would have to push hard to make our daily goal. I knew it would take at least four days to get from start to finish. At the age of 60, I didn't know how long I'd have the stamina. This was the time to go for it.

There was one fear that haunted me--mountain lions. I had heard stories of attacks. It usually happened to people that were in the woods alone. The thought of being stalked and always watching my back made my blood run cold. Sleeping at night in a little light tent with predators on the prowl, I'm sure I would not have gotten much rest. A shiver ran down my spine at the thought. But I also heard mountain lions were shy and would rather sneak off whenever humans were around. It would be just my luck that I would encounter the one that wasn't shy.

I would feel safer with someone else around. Most of my friends were my age or older and just laughed at me when I asked them. Most just said I was crazy to take on such an aggressive hike at my age. With August as a target date, there were plenty of good days to get into condition. I needed someone soon so they could also have time to get into condition. Finding a walking partner took time.

One day it came to me. I knew a young man that could use this trip as much as me. He had lost his mother. It could be good for both of us. So the next day I asked him.

"Hey, Brian, I'm planning on walking the Mickelson Trail and I need a hiking partner. How would you like to go with me?"

"Dad, are you nuts? Man, I can't believe you'd even think about something that crazy. That trail is over a 100 miles."

"Brian, I'm going with or without you."

As Brian walked away shaking his head, it was obvious he knew this would be more than a walk in the park.

That ended the conversation for a few days. He needed time to think it over before I sprung it on him again.

Back when Patricia's condition got worse, Brian came to live in the basement to help me care for her. After our loss, he stayed, but we didn't talk much because we were both in our own world of grief.

I left the information all over the table giving Brian the impression that I would go it alone. My strategy worked. A few days later, Brian said "Okay, I'll go with you because someone needs to keep an eye on my crazy old man."

Brian had a close bond with his mom. Ever since he was little he would go to her rather than me for things and to talk. They seemed to think alike on so many subjects. When Brian lost her, he lost his biggest supporter. She was his guiding lighthouse. After that his pathway went dark.

I was so caught up in my own grief; I couldn't see how much he was hurting. I blamed myself for so many reasons why Brian and I weren't that close. I probably spent more time chewing him out then praising him on his accomplishments. Maybe I said no far too many times to things he asked for. As a dad I could have done better. Hopefully we can improve our relationship.

As a boy, Brian loved taking old VCRs and other things apart just to see what made them tick. I guess we both have a curious nature.

Brian's brown eyes came from his mother. There is some comfort in seeing some of Patricia's traits in my kids. That way part of her lives on.

My son and I have a similar build, except I have more padding around the mid-section. Maybe we can look more like twins if I walk off the mid bulge.

So the WHO on my plan list was checked off. Next was the HOW MUCH. We began to make up a packing list. When you hike, the weight of the things you carry becomes an issue. First, Brian and I needed some good lightweight backpacks with plenty of room for our essentials. So what did we need? Water bottles were a must, and power bars for food and energy. I knew there were water stations about every ten miles and a number of towns along the way. We could stop for a bigger meal once a day and that would be good enough for us.

A couple of lightweight tents were the answer to our lodging. Okay, food, water, lodging, next we looked for hygiene stuff. I found some small soap bars and Brian found something real cool, a packet of tiny tooth brushes with a bead of tooth paste already on them, and the other end was a tooth pick. That would save both weight and space.

I planned to take pictures along the way, so I bought a small digital camera. For journaling as I went along, I got a little notebook and pen.

So what about protection? I didn't feel confident with a gun or a knife. I'd probably shoot myself in the foot or cut myself.

We went to a sports store to get some ideas for protection. In bear country, they sold a pepper spray. It could shoot a stream up to 20 feet. If it could stop a bear, surely it could stop a mountain lion.

On the internet, it showed what to do if you encountered a mountain lion. If you waved your hands in the air with a jacket or something it makes you look bigger. They hate loud noises, so if you yell or holler or bang on something like a pan it can drive them off. The worst thing you could do is turn and run. That makes you look like prey.

Mountain lions are kind of like life's problems, if you face them, you can be victorious, but if you turn and run from life's problems, they can overtake you.

As we looked over our backpacks and supplies, it hit me. This isn't just a dream anymore; we're really going to do this. This was something I wanted to do ever since I was a kid. A shudder of anticipation ran down my spine. Within me, I felt the energy of my youth welling up deep inside. Even with the ups and downs of my emotions, it felt good to let my soul dance for at least a little while.

I hoped Brian would get caught up in the excitement and not just go to watch over me. He didn't always say what was on his mind. That made him a little hard to read. When it came to our grief, I wonder if we'll ever be able to talk about it.

CHAPTER SIX

There were days when things were going well, and then BANG, I was ambushed with painful emotions. It didn't take much. Just a song I heard, a smell, or anything that would remind me of the one I had lost. The support group calls these emotional ambushes "triggers."

One day all it took for me to get depressed was a cloudy day. The dreariness brought an old song to mind, 'Ain't No Sunshine When She's Gone.' Well, my sunshine was gone and would never return.

That put my mind in a very dark place. It took me to a gut-wrenching mournful spot. No one really understands this grievous place unless they had been there. I began to imagine walking on thin ice on a winter's pond. I was alone. There was no one with in miles that could hear my screams for help. Fear penetrated my bones. As I stepped forward, I could hear the sickening sound of cracking ice. Suddenly the ice gave way and I was plunged into the cold dark waters of despair. It was a continuous fight just to keep my head above the surface. The ice at the edge of the hole kept breaking away, making it almost impossible to get out. Finally, I was back up on the ice, but I was exhausted. After a while, I got up on my feet and started walking again. Crash, down I went again, there was no strength left in me. Should I just give up and sink slowly and quietly into the cold, deep, dark, depts. of depression? The horror of it all shook me.

"Okay Jim, snap out of it!" I had to give myself a strong pep talk each time I fell into depression. It was hard to pick myself up again and move forward.

It was time to reach into my emotional toolbox and do some repair with the tools from the toolbox I received from my grief support group. The first tool was to remind me that Patricia was in Glory, a place where nothing could harm her ever again. It's a place of peace and no pain, a destination where the very presence of GOD lights up the place. Some day when GOD calls me home, I'll see her again at a place of no goodbyes.

The next tool reminded me that, with help, someday the pain will not be so intense. Pain can be replaced by treasured memories. In the early part of the grief journey, I couldn't see that as a possibility. The darkness in the valley covered the pathway ahead so where was the brighter future?

The ups and downs of grief were exhausting. Sometimes, if I just broke down and cried, I felt better. Other times, some soothing music helped. Little breaks from the journey of grief, for instance, a friend taking me out to lunch, also helped me cope.

If I focused on something positive, like the big hike, that helped take my mind off my troubles. There were so many details to work out.

One of the details for the trip was where to leave the vehicle while we were on the trail. Also we needed someone to drop us off at the starting point and pick us up at the end of the trail. It just so happened that my sister and her husband, Gayle and Tim Tescher, lived in the beautiful town of Hot Springs in the southern Black Hills.

One evening, I gave them a call. They were happy to hear we were coming for a visit, but I wondered what they thought about our crazy plan. Even if they thought we were nuts, they were very supportive.

We chose the days and times that were most convenient for them. If it weren't for the help of Tim and Gayle, I wonder if we could have even made it to the hills to start such a journey. They were so gracious.

Now we had an actual day and time to prepare for. The wheels were turning. Sometimes I felt guilty about enjoying life after my loss, like I wasn't honoring her memory. Then I remembered what she said to me. To heal was the best way to honor her, and I needed to keep my promise.

Brian and I would strap on our backpacks and go for walks. We started out light, and then increased the load each day until we figured it was about the weight we would be carrying. As we walked, I could imagine the pine trees and babbling brooks along the way. My leg muscles felt stronger as we got closer to the big day.

Looking at the map, it was easy to see that starting at Deadwood was the best way to go, because it would be more downhill for us. Deadwood was in the northern Black Hills and Edgemont was on the plains, just beyond the southern foot hills.

Another detail that needed to be worked out was dog care. Rufus and Rosey were used to routine. I lined up a friend to stop by the house to take them out three times a day and feed them. It needed to be someone they knew, someone that loved animals and would spend a little time with them. They always ate at the same time each day, and got a treat if they were good dogs. My closest friend, Duane, stepped up to the plate for me. I knew he loved animals. I knew the dogs would be in good hands.

We had a spare bedroom to keep all our supplies together for the trip. The packing list kept growing, but we had to be careful not to over pack for the hike.

August was usually a dry month, so we couldn't build any campfires along the way. That meant no cooking supplies. I didn't feel like dragging pots and pans in my backpack any-way. It wouldn't bother us to eat trail-mix as we moved down the trail. Besides, there would be no dishes or clean-up. I liked that also.

Over and over, I kept thinking about what would be neces-sary for the trip. I also checked with Brian to see if he thought of anything.

A pair of small LED flashlights was also a must. They needed to be bright enough to keep us from stumbling in the dark. Oh yes, a basic first aid kit is always a good idea just in case of an emergency. If we missed anything that should have been on the list, we could pick it up in one of the towns along the trail.

There was one load we wished we didn't have to take with us. If only we could have left it home. No matter where we went, grief was a heavy weight on our shoulders. If it had been possible

I would have dug it out of my backpack and stuffed it under my bed. In reality, I knew that was impossible. I just hoped this trip could lighten the load a little.

CHAPTER SEVEN

Day after day Brian and I walked to get into condition. The day before the big trip I had jitters of anticipation. The feeling reminded me of playing baseball as a kid who was coming up to the plate with bat in hand and bases loaded. I wanted to be the hero in my own life. I needed to prove to myself that I was more than a beaten down widower. We were ready to knock this trip out of the park.

There were a few things to wrap up before we hit the road. I stopped the mail and paper while we were gone. I knew my friend Duane would keep an eye on things around the house and care for the dogs.

One more time before the trip, Brian and I spread the map out on the table to look it over. The Mickelson Trail was marked by red dashes that zig-zagged though the center of the Black Hills.

As I ran my finger along the dashes I stated "the trail is 109 miles long. If we could divide this hike into fourths, that would be a little over 27 miles a day. It would be nice if each night we ended up by a town to get a warm meal before we camp out. The problem is the last two legs of the trail are longer because there are fewer towns and trail heads. We will have to cover more miles to reach our stopping points."

"Hey Dad, can you handle 30 plus miles in one day?"

"Are you kidding, I just hope you can keep up with me," I piped back.

I didn't want Brian to know I had my doubts about the last two legs of the trail and my own two legs making it. I hoped my poker face and upbeat response was convincing.

We had determined that Deadwood in the northern hills was our starting point. Following the red marked trail with my finger, I came to Rochford.

"It looks like Rochford is most likely our first stop for the night."

"Okay, why Rochford, can't we go a little farther?"

"First of all, they have a bar and grill. It would be nice if we have a warm meal before bedding down. There is no place to eat until we get all the way to Hill City. There is no way we can get there without traveling in the dark. The train tunnels are past Rochford and I don't want to go through them at night."

"I get it Dad, so Rochford it is. Maybe if we get up early enough we can grab breakfast before we leave."

"Great idea, a good warm meal would give us an extra boost."

It was hard to judge miles between stops because of the winding trail. The zig-zagging added more miles than going straight from point A to point B.

"I estimate it's about 20 miles from Deadwood to Rochford."

Brian looked closer at the map, "Okay, the next night should put us about here." He pointed to Hill City.

"You're right on; it should be about 25miles between Rochford and Hill City. They probably have a campground with a sanitation station with a restroom and showers. There would be a number of good restaurants we can choose from."

"That should take care of the 2nd night. The next town would be Custer."

"The problem is it would only take about half a day to get there."

"Okay, Dad, then we keep moving on. There is nothing until we get to Pringle. That looks like quite a stretch."

"I'm guessing around 30 miles. There is a lodge there that I heard serves some great burgers. Hey Brian, get this! If we eat breakfast before leaving Hill City, then we can have lunch at Custer, and finish with supper at Pringle--that would be three square meals in one day. I just hope we don't put on more calories than we burn off!" Brian nodded with a chuckle.

"That should be the 3rd and last night of sleeping under the stars. Day four should be the home stretch to Edgemont. Man! Look at that distance between Pringle and Edgemont! There are no towns along the way. How far do you think it is, Dad?"

"It's got to be close to 35 miles. Now do you see why I said the last two legs of the trail would be the longest? There are two more things to consider. It would be wise if we get some trail mix and other food in Hill City to eat on the last leg of the hike. As you see there are no places along the way to grab a bite. Next we have to get to Edgemont before sunset. It's dangerous at night. Poisonous rattlesnakes like to hunt in the dark. It would be hard to see them. I'd hate to step on one of those devils. I shudder to think of a snake bite in the dark with no help for miles."

"Also it would be nice to have some light for photographs at the finish line."

"So Brian, do you think we have a good plan?"

"Ah, well, I guess I'm up for the challenge."

It was time to load the pickup. We needed to have some clothes for the stay over at Tim and Gayle's place. Our backpacks were ready. With the pickup loaded we were prepared for an early start in the morning.

Brian and I wanted to stop at a few places along the way to the Black Hills. An early start would give us more time to sightsee. We planned to take the loop through the Badlands, a geological formation formed by erosion. I remember taking the family there when the kids were small. I also remember my parents taking us kids there. We have generations of memories in the Badlands.

At the end of the loop, we will come to Wall Drug. There are signs all over the world stating how far it is to Wall Drug. It is world renowned. It would be fun to see it again.

In the early 30's Ted and Dorothy Hustead bought a drugstore in Wall, South Dakota. It's located on the west edge of the Badlands.

The first few years' business was slow. Most the traffic just zipped by. If things hadn't picked up they might have to close.

Ted and Dorothy came up with a plan to offer free ice water. Ted put up signs along the highway promoting ice water and the thirsty travelers began to pour in.

As they drank free ice water, they bought ice cream and souvenirs.

Wall Drug is now a regular stopping place for thousands of tourists each year. You can get five cent coffee and oh yes, free ice water. The place has really grown since its beginnings. The main street of Wall bustles with shops and restaurants.

I went over my checklist:

Pick-up loaded

Oil

Belts

Tires

Fill gas tank

It was time for the dogs to go out before bedtime. Now, I was ready for a good night's sleep.

"Dad, have we ever done anything this big together before?"

"Man, I don't know, but it's got to be at the top of the list."

"Good night, Brian see yah in the morning."

"Night Dad, sleep tight.".

CHAPTER EIGHT

At the crack of dawn, I popped out of bed ready for the big day. Brian was not a morning person. I wanted to get an early start, but what if Brian slept in?

"Hey, Brian, you up?" I yelled down the stairs.

"Let me sleep a little longer," he moaned.

"Darn it, Brian, I was afraid of this."

"Relax, Dad, I'm just messing with you, I'm up. I'll be upstairs in a couple minutes."

With that response, I paced the floor. That's what I did when I got impatient. Brian and I are so different. He is so laid-back and I'm a go-dog-go type person. My hit-the-road-a-running attitude sometimes drives Brian nuts. Sure hope it doesn't cause problems on the trip.

I checked on things around the house, watered plants, made sure the dogs had plenty of water, and made a last look at the packing list. One more thing before we headed out the door. I needed to have a talk with the dogs. Some people may think I'm crazy, but they understand more than you think.

"Okay Rufus, Rosie, Duane will come and let you out and feed you. You be good dogs. Let's go out one more time before the trip. Sorry, but you guys stay. You aren't coming with us."

After the dogs took care of business, I locked the door knowing Duane had my spare key and cellphone number. We were all set.

Brian and I were greeted by the fresh morning air as we approached the vehicle. "Man! What a perfect day." Taking a deep breath, I settled in behind the wheel.

First things first, a place to eat and a good cup of coffee before we leave town, I had to have my coffee. With a good breakfast and a cup to go, we were on our way.

The whole map was laid out in my head. Hwy 37 south to 34 west, then the short cut to Interstate 90 by way of Hwy 47 from Fort Thompson to Reliance. Once on I-90 we just go west to the hills.

"Hey, guess what, Brian? We gain an hour at Murdo." Today the time zone is our friend.

As we headed down I- 90, Brian piped up, "How about some travel music?" Brian and I didn't always enjoy the same types of music so we found a compromise. With me at the wheel and my sidekick playing the tuner, soon we were jamming to the tunes. Like a couple of coyotes howling at the moon, we felt on top of the world.

A thought ambushed me. An angry inner voice screamed. What the hell are you doing? You lost a wife, Brian lost a mother. Shame on you! You should be mourning her loss. How dare you act like nothing happened?

Brian noticed I stopped singing.

"You okay Dad?"

"Sure, just fine," I replied as I pasted on a smile.

Why should that nasty voice kill both our moods?

Then a familiar voice came into my head, a softer, kinder voice.

It's okay, I'm fine up here in Glory. "You made a promise to work on the pain of loss and a promise to heal. I'm proud of you guys. Keep it up. Someday we'll be together again."

At the next chorus, I joined in again. It's gonna be a great day.

Past Kadoka, we turned south into the Badlands National Park. This road is a loop that will take us through the best of the Badlands to Cedar Pass, then near the town of Interior, and returns to Interstate 90, and Wall Drug.

As Brian and I drove along, clay formations caught our attention. We couldn't just zip through the Badlands because there were scenic views that could take one's breath away.

Despite the beauty of the Badlands, it can be an unforgiving place, a place that shows no mercy. In the summer temperatures can rise to over a 100 degrees. The clay makes this land an oven. With little water, it's like a desert of clay-covered hills. Definitely not a place you want to get lost.

Some days my grief felt like I was a poor soul, lost wondering around out there, and no water to quench my parched body. Buzzards were circling up above, just waiting for my impending doom. Okay, that's enough; I can't keep focusing on my grief. Oh Lord! Can't I put my grief aside for a little while? Give me a break.

Soon we came to Cedar Pass. It had a visitor's center with a restaurant, so we wandered through the exhibits and then sat down to a nice meal. The logs and timbers with rock walls made the place so rustic and beautiful.

A bittersweet emotion welled up in my chest. Patricia would have loved this place. I choked up. With a drink of water, I swallowed my feelings deep within so Brian wouldn't notice. Finally, I managed to mention it was time to move on; there was still a lot to see before the day was over.

Continuing down the winding road felt like a different world. The rugged hills of clay were gray with reddish stripes. They made all kinds of formations, like round haystacks or stately castles reaching for the sky. I could imagine the strange ancient creatures that used to roam this area. I got a glimpse of what they may have looked like from the fossils we had seen at the exhibits.

I noticed some wildlife on a hillside. Big horn sheep, mountain goats, and antelope roam the landscape these days.

"This place brings back a lot of memories of family trips."

"For sure, Dad, I'm glad we took those breaks to enjoy life. I wish things could go back to the way they ------"

Brian stopped talking and looked away. An awkward silence ended the conversation. I wished he could have finished the sentence. Maybe we needed to get it out in the open, but we didn't feel like talking about our pain at that time. It was easier to ignore each other's emotions rather than dealing with them.

Eventually I broke the silence with, "This is a great place for photography. Sunrises and sunsets bring out the colors of the formations."

Brian nodded in agreement.

Leaving the Badlands behind, we pulled into the town of Wall. I was ready for some cold water and five cent coffee. The place bustled with tourists shopping for souvenirs. We had fun looking at all the rock shops, Black Hills Gold, and tee shirt shops. We could have stayed longer, but we needed to get to Hot Springs before dark.

It was Brian's turn at the wheel. We were now on I-90 again.

Soon the western horizon began to change. The level sky line began to ripple. It was the first glimpse of the Black Hills. At Rapid City, we turned south on Hwy 79 along the eastern edge of the Hills. Eventually around Hwy 18 we really got into the splendor of the southern part of the hills. Rolling down the windows, we were greeted by the sweet smell of the magnificent pines. Tall red cliffs broke up the landscape. What a contrast to the flat prairie! After all our preparation, it felt good to finally be here in the hills.

Around a few bends in the road and tucked in a cozy canyon was the historic town of Hot Springs. This was the home of Evan's Plunge and the Mammoth Digs, (an archeological mammoth site.) Also, on a hillside stood the Veteran's Home with its peaceful surroundings. Many of the buildings we saw were built over a 100 years ago. People used to travel great distances for the hot springs that they felt had healing powers.

We were greeted with open arms, as we arrived at Tim and Gayle's. We were finally there.

CHAPTER NINE

The chatter with Tim and Gayle around the supper table was full of anticipation. It was so refreshing to look ahead to the trail, instead of behind me at all my sadness. I spent way too much time in the past tense. I was bound to stumble, if I kept looking back while I tried to move forward.

Brian and I were so pumped up about this big adventure that we bombarded them with all kinds of questions about the trail. They had lived in Hot Springs for quite a while. One of their favorite pastimes was traveling the back roads of the hills on their motorcycles. Many times they crossed over the Mickelson Trail or coasted alongside on a parallel road.

Tim said, "The trail is a peace of heaven. It's a great place to unwind. There are old cabins and building from the Gold Rush Days. The trail has a lot of history."

Gayle added, "Yes, it is a beautiful trail, but remember, because of the landscape, you will go through many cell phone dead zones. At times it will be just you and Brian, no contact with civilization. Please be careful."

Tim nodded, "Also no motor vehicles are allowed on the trail so if you walk into the Hills you have to walk out."

After an evening of trail talk and getting caught up on the family news it was time to retire for the night.

Before we went to bed, Brian and I checked our backpacks and supplies again. Okay, I think we're ready. It's lights out.

The smell of bacon and eggs greeted us as we got out of bed the next morning with a cup of coffee awaited me, the best cup of the day. Because it was Sunday morning, we dressed up for church. Faith has always been an important part of my family's life. That morning I prayed for God's guiding hand on the trail. After church we ate out, and then changed into our hiking clothes. It was time for Tim and Gayle to drop us off at Deadwood in the northern hills.

As we drove, I tried to imagine what was behind those beautiful hills. The trail goes to places not seen from the road. My boyhood adventurous spirit surfaced within me. I'd always wondered what was over the next hill or what was around the next bend. For a while I was lost in my imagination. I couldn't count the times I walked that trail in my dreams. It was about to get real. I must have dozed off because it seemed like the car grew wings and in no time we were pulling into Deadwood.

First, we needed to check into a motel. The place we found had the Mickelson Trail right in its backyard.

After Tim and Gayle wished us well and dropped us off, Brian and I settled into our room.

"Hey Dad," Let's check out Deadwood."

"Yeah," We have all afternoon to snoop around downtown, right?"

We stepped onto the Mickelson Trail to head downtown. It felt like stepping onto the yellow brick road. I wasn't worried about lions, tigers, or bears, oh my. There haven't been any sightings of witches or flying monkeys. So we're off to see...ah Deadwood.

After rounding the corner, we entered the city park. That's where the northern part of the railroad ends. A little steam engine sat on the track in an open shed. We saw other railroad equipment from days gone by. As we wandered into the park, two other people came along. Brian and I asked if they could take some pictures of us at the beginning of the trail. After that we told them about what we planned to do. Handing back the camera, they smiled, shook their heads, and said good luck. Then they just walked away muttering something we couldn't hear.

After they left, I turned to Brian, "They think we're nuts."

We locked eyes and he replied," Maybe we are."

I started to laugh and he joined in.

A little twinge of doubt struck me, but I couldn't show fear now. We'd come this far. I tended to wait for the next thing to go wrong. What could go wrong in a beautiful place like the Black Hills? Shaking off the uneasy feeling, I moved on.

Passing all the casinos, reminded me of a time when this town was untamed. Western legends walked this town. Wild Bill Hickok and Calamity Jane were two of the best known characters of their time. I could almost feel them following us down the street. Some people believe there are a few hotels in the area that are haunted. The stories of Wild Bill must have left an impact on me as a kid, because I still don't like to turn my back to the door in a restaurant when I eat.

There was a photo shop where one could get an old-time style photo taken in old western clothes and sit by an old pot belly stove or in a saloon backdrop. Then the photo was made to look aged. Patricia and I did that once. I sat in an old rocker with a rifle across my lap and she stood up straight behind me with her hand on my shoulder. She wore something lacy and a fancy hat. I was in buckskins. We had to be poker faced. I've never seen anyone smile in an old photograph.

In a nearby grocery store we got some trail mix for the journey. Before heading back to the motel, we found a nice restaurant to fuel up for the trip. In the morning, the plan was to have a continental breakfast before heading out. Maybe we'll grab an apple or something for the road.

Looking at my watch I said, "Well it's time to get back to the motel."

"Really, why do old people think about bed before the sun goes down?"

I hunched my back, squinted my eyes, looked up over my glasses at Brian, and in an old man shaky voice I responded.

"We have a long day tomorrow; I want to be rested up for it."

With that we headed back to the motel to bed down for the night. As I settled in to call it a day, I knew my mind would be walking part of the trail again. I just hoped I wouldn't dream about mountain lions.

CHAPTER TEN

Brian and I were up before dawn. The sun was casting its light over the eastern ridge as we fueled up on a continental breakfast and juice. With a cup of coffee in my hand, it was the start of a perfect day. We were ready to take on the world.

I leaned towards Brian and said, "Wow, we are really here. We are doing this. With all the planning, preparation, and anticipation, we are actually doing this. The big day is finally here."

With a smirk Brian replied "Dad, do you think you could show a little more enthusiasm."

"I get it, very funny, Brian."

After gathering our stuff and checking out, we headed on a short jaunt to the Mickelson Trail.

"Wow! It's the beginning of the adventure of a lifetime."

"Yeah Dad, this is the big day, just don't let the mountain lions get you."

"That's not funny," I retorted as I checked to see if my pepper spray was secured to my belt.

He laughed, "It'll be fine, you'll see".

An eagle screeched high in the sky as if to say "I have my eye on you." That was a reminder that God Almighty always has an eye on us. We were first time hikers and there were so many unknowns ahead of us. A list of (what ifs) came to mind. What if one of us broke a leg? What if we got hit by a falling rock? The isolation of not having any other humans around was daunting, but the thought of God's omnipotent presence gave me comfort. Why should I fear? Shouldn't my faith be bigger than my fear?

My thought was broken by a chipmunk scampering across the path right in front of me. It stopped only long enough to take a last look at us before vanishing into the brush.

Just outside of town, the trail led us to the base of a deep gorge with tall cliffs towering over us on two sides. The trail had been wonderfully maintained. I liked the fact that the path was packed gravel and not asphalt or cement. It made it a lot easier on the feet.

The towering cliffs made us feel so small in comparison to our surroundings. It felt like the tall banks rolled back like giant theater curtains exposing a grand panoramic view. Behind us we could no longer see civilization. We were on our own. At that point, I realized we were the only two people on earth that were looking at this fantastic sight.

"Brian, stop a minute and look around. Have you ever seen any place like this?"

"Not that I can think of, Dad, this is amazing."

It was like a lost canyon, a place very few people have seen. The towering red cliffs with vegetation hanging off them and crowned with pine trees made me feel like I was in an adventure movie. No postcard could come close to this splendor.

At the base of the gorge, the only way to the top was to follow the bottom as it wandered back and forth. We struggled as the incline became steeper. It was a real test of our endurance. Good thing we got conditioned for this.

"Can you imagine the power it took to get a steam engine up this gorge with its load? Think of all those tons of steel, iron ore, and timbers that had to be pulled up to the top.

Brian responded, "Maybe it took three or four engines hooked together to get the job done."

"Yeah, that would make sense."

We climbed the trail until it began to level off a little. My legs began to weaken and I was panting like a dog.

"Hey, Brian, can we stop a minute? I need to catch my breath."

"Sure Dad, if you have to."

I think Brian needed a break too; he just didn't want me to see it. After a few minutes I was ready to push on.

Soon the sound of a soothing chatter from a sparkling stream reached our ears. I imaged it as the background music of nature with the birds of the air carrying the main melody. They sang a song older then the hills. Yet it still had the power to melt some of my fears and lift my spirits. It was such a peaceful place. It was everything Tim said it was and more.

I was so caught up in the beauty. I hadn't noticed that Brian was dropping behind.

"Hey, Brian, you better catch up. We need to get to Rochford before nightfall."

He muttered something back which I didn't quite hear.

I yelled a little louder, "Brian, when we get there, we need to eat and then pitch our tents. We don't want to try to pitch our tents in the dark."

"Dad, he yelled back, "If you don't slow down and pace yourself, you'll be shot before you make it halfway!"

He was right. With my experience as a 5k runner, I learned to saves some energy for the finish. It was hard to slow down because I had so much adrenalin built up inside.

After lagging back a little longer, Brian stopped and dug a small MP3 player out of his backpack. Putting in his earpiece, he started walking again. In no time he caught up with me. Soon he was leaving me in the dust.

"Brian, slow down. Pace yourself. Darn it, wait for me!"

He couldn't hear me because of the noise in his ear.

"I hope your battery dies!" I yelled.

There was still no response.

A little farther down the road, we finally found our stride. While Brian listened to his tunes, I continued to listen to the songs of nature. The sounds of the birds, the whisper of the breeze through the pine trees are all music to my ears. To me, it was God's creation putting on a concert.

Up to our right, on top of the hill, there stood the tower for the Homestake Gold Mine. The mine started up in1878 and ran until it closed in 2002. It was the largest and deepest gold mine in North America. In 2007 it was reopened as a deep underground science and engineering laboratory. One of the research projects is the study of dark matter. When I looked it up, it was described as a form thought to account for approximately 85% of matter in the universe and about 27% of its total mass-energy. Well, that sure cleared things up for me. It's too deep and too dark to understand.

Along the way, we noticed the square stone post mile markers. As we headed south, the numbers grew smaller. The first markers made us feel overwhelmed. They reminded us that we had more than 100 miles to go. The walk was more like a countdown.

At some point we got a break from the climbing. The pathway was level and straight.

An old shack by the side of the trail caught my eye. It was unusual because the roof and the siding were covered with flattened tin can lids. A plaque at the site said the lids were from chemical containers that were used to process the gold at the mine. What a clever way to make shingles and siding. It still sheds rain to this day.

The trail began to climb again to the highest point of the journey. The beauty of the hills was glorious. Every now and then, we would have to stop and take it all in. This was the best time, in mid-August, to walk the trail because we could pick ripe wild raspberries along the way. These little bushes no bigger than a tomato plant were loaded with their juicy fruit. They gave us that little extra lift we needed to get to our trailhead.

To our surprise, we came upon the first tunnel-Tunnel D. I thought all the tunnels were on the other side of Rochford. To think, years back, trains passed through this tunnel. I could tell the place was safe. All the timber in the shoring was new. Brian and I had never walked through a mountain before. It wasn't very long so we could see the light at the other side. A fresh breeze met us as we entered. I studied the marks on the walls and roof from the tools used to chisel through the mountain. The timbers that shored things up were massive. About half way through we stopped to look behind us and ahead.

"Brian, we are now in the middle of a mountain."

"This is definitely a first"

After one last look at the tunnel's exit, it was time to push on. Our legs were getting tired and hunger was setting in. The thought of a nice warm meal awaiting us compelled us to trudge forward.

We reached Rochford with two hours of daylight to spare. There was time to go to the little town to eat. The burger and fries at the Moonshine Gulch were so much better than from some fast food place. There were 100's of baseball caps hanging from the ceiling. They were donated from tourists that came here from all over the States and even from other countries   I was told that some weekends this can be a hopping place. Local bands would entertain here.

"Now this is the life, a big juicy burger in one hand and a cup of coffee in the other, can it get any better than this?"

"Dad, winning the lottery could be a close second."

After a good meal, it was back to the trailhead campsite. We set up the tents and prepared for a good night's sleep.

"What a day, right Brian? We climbed a gorge and walked through a mountain."

"Yes, it was an incredible day, but I'm ready to call it a night."

Even though we had a good day on the trail, as I settled into my tent, that nagging, uneasy, gut- feeling came back to me. Things were going too smoothly. Tragedy is like a mountain lion following us, just waiting for the right time to attack. We may not have known what calamity awaited Brian and me, but I could feel something was about to move in on us.

CHAPTER ELEVEN

A gentle cool breeze whispered through the pine trees. We grabbed our light jackets before entering our tents. "This should be some good sleeping weather,"   I thought as I settled in for the night. My little LED flashlight was clipped to my backpack so I could find it in the night if I needed it. Finding a soft spot on my pack, I used it as a pillow.

"Good night, sleep tight."

"Yeah, night."

My mind began to wonder back to the beautiful rugged landscape we saw along the way. The Mickelson Trail did not disappoint me. I had to shake off that gut-feeling, I was just a little paranoid. There was adventure around every corner. Soon I drifted off to sleep.

In the middle of the night, I woke up. Something was wrong. I was damp. A chill ran down my back. As I reached for my flashlight, a shower of icy water fell on me. "What the heck? Now I'm just plain wet. Is it raining? Do I have a hole in my tent? There wasn't any rain in the forecast." I zipped open the tent and peeked out. Cold night air hit me in the face. Stars glistened in the cloudless sky. "So why am I wet?" As I retreated back in to my tent, I shined the light up on the ceiling. There was my answer. The ceiling was covered with cold sparkling water droplets. "Darn! Condensation." Cold air outside, body heat inside, and a nylon tent to trap in the moisture spelled disaster.

My body shivered uncontrollably. My teeth chattered so hard I thought I'd chip them. Who would have thought it would get down to the low forties or lower in mid-August? I didn't take into account the fact that we were at 5000 feet attitude. We were not prepared for this. To make matters worse, campfires were prohibited so we didn't bring anything to build one. Also, there was no signal for cell phones. We were in a dead zone.

Things just kept getting worse. I was starting to cramp up from hours of shivering. Each time I stretched out my legs, I touched the side of the tent and got another cold shower.

This situation had all the makings of hypothermia. People can die from it. First the body temp drops, then the nervous system shuts down and the shivering stops. Then the victim gets sleepy and falls asleep. That's when the breathing and heart stop. After that you're a goner.

I would hate to have my epitaph say: Jim died of hypothermia in mid-August in South Dakota. It would look like I got stuck in a cooler or something. This just can't happen.

Where can I find heat? All that's left is body heat. That's it! Body heat, Brian and I can combine our body heat.

"Oh no!" I hadn't heard a peep from Brian's tent all night.

"Brian, are you okay?"

"I'm freezing," came a weak response.

"We are now in survival mode. The only heat we have is our body heat; Brian, I'm coming in."

"Hell no! Dad."

Brian had never been much of a hugger, and I being up next to him in a small tent was an invasion of his space. I knew I needed to use the old guilt trip to get in.

"Okay, Brian, if you find me dead in the morning, you would know that you could have done something but didn't. You would have to live with that the rest of your life."

"You can come in under one condition, if we lie down back to back. If an arm comes over me, I'm out of here."

"Okay, I get it."

As I zipped open the tent, more condensation fell on Brian who responded with a few choice words.

Neither one of us wanted to close our eyes. We had seen too many movies where victims never woke up. The rest of the night was spent shivering and waiting for daylight. As much as we hated shivering, it would be worse if it stopped. That would be the beginning of the end. It would be so embarrassing to have markers put up that said; this is the site where two amateur hikers froze to death in cheap tents in mid-August. We have to survive!

Finally, daylight broke through the horrible night, and we were still alive. As we staggered the short distance to Rochford for breakfast at the Moonshine Gulch, we hoped it would be open. To our relief, the unlocked screen door squeaked as we opened it.

The chef came from the back room in her apron with spatula in hand. "What'll it be, boys?" The smell of bacon and eggs soon filled the air. The sizzle on the grill was music to my ears, and oh yes, the coffee! I wrapped my cold fingers around that heavenly warm cup, breathed in that out of this world aroma, and sipped the warm fantastic liquid. It felt good to be alive! It's surprising how a good breakfast can lift ones spirits.

With a bite of bacon, I spoke up. "You know what? I think we can still do this."

"Nope, I'm done," Brian responded.

"Brian, The sun is out and it can warm us up and dry us out. We are going down in altitude. In Hill City they probably have a campground, and we can get some of those chemical heating pads for the night. I know we c—

"Hell no, I'm done." Brian responded.

Again I tried to make him reconsider, "You know, after we get back on the trail, all we need to do is lean forward, put one foot before the other, repeat the process, and we are on our way."

"Dad, what part of no don't you understand?

As Brian tried to control his emotions, he lowered his voice and leaned closer toward me. To emphasize his point, he spoke slowly and clearly.

"I will not spend another night in that tent. There is a pay phone on the porch. I am going to call Tim and Gayle to come get me. If you want to keep going, go ahead, but you'll have to go it alone."

Brian called and Gayle was on her way. I knew it was over for me too. After only one day on the trail, and only 20 miles, it was over. I felt like the boy who came up to bat, bases loaded, last inning, and the whole game was on my shoulders. With three strikes I let everyone down. The walk back to camp was in silence. We had nothing more to say to each other.

It was time to disassemble those stupid cheap tents. I was tempted to just leave them with a sign that said, FREE. But it's always the right thing to clean up after ourselves. I didn't want to feel bad about leaving junk behind.

When Gayle came, she didn't have to ask, "Hey guys, how's it going?" Just one look at us told her we were haggard. I tried to give some kind of apology. I felt terrible that she had to take some time off work to come get us. She probably told them she had to go rescue a couple of amateur hikers in the high county.

The trip back to Hot Springs was pretty quiet. Depression came over me like a dark fog, choking out the light. All I could think about was all the plans and preparation that went into this trip. I'm a failure, a loser. I was in another one of my pity parties and no one else was invited.

The first thing I did when we got back to Hot Springs was to take a nice warm shower and laid down. I don't know how long I rested, but when I woke up the question came to mind, now what? Maybe tomorrow I'll walk around Hot Springs and check out the stores, etc.

After Tim and Gayle returned from work, we had supper. Things seemed a little strained, because Brian and I weren't on speaking terms. In fact, we made very little eye contact. "This trip was supposed to help us bond, not drive us apart," I told myself. After sharing a few highlights of the hike, I said goodnight.

CHAPTER TWELVE

Morning came and I knew I was in a bad mood. I did not want to be around cheerful people. I wanted to wallow in self- pity like a hog in mud. Just let me cover myself with depression, defeat, and all the other emotions that come with being a loser.

I told Gayle she didn't need to put on the coffee pot for me. The plan was to sleep- in to recover from all the sleep we missed the night before. The house was quiet when I got up. Tim and Gayle went off to work and Brian was probably still in bed. He could sleep all day for all I cared.

My stomach was growling, so it was time to head downtown to get a bite and a cup of coffee. The house was on the south ridge, so I walked to University Avenue and started the descent to the main street. This seemed to fit my mood, all downhill from here.

There was a convenient store with breakfast burritos and a fresh pot of coffee just waiting for me. With a few sips I felt like I could talk to someone without biting their head off.

As I strolled downtown, I saw a senior veteran in a wheelchair rolling along. Someone called his name and with a big smile and a wave he responded back. When he got to the curb, the traffic stopped both ways and patiently let him cross. I'd heard about the locals of Hot Springs watching out for their vets. This incident confirmed to me the caring attitude of the community. When I saw that veteran and the kindness shown to him, my bad mood started to melt away.

There were some antique shops that were filled with cool stuff. I had plenty of time to look around. Up on the north ridge stood an old two story stone school house that overlooked the gorge. It was made from the same quarry rock as so many of the other buildings in town. The well- kept old structures made me feel like I had stepped back in time. The old school house was now converted into a museum. To get to it there was a long cement stairway. The climb was good exercise. There was so much history in the area, I spent quite a while taking it all in.

Before heading back down the stairs I stopped to look at the town from that elevated vantage point. Man, what a view! When I was downtown I could only see what was around me, but from up here I could see so much more. It made me think of what things might look like from God's vantage point. In life I could only see what affected me, but from God's vantage point, He is able to see so much more. He can ever see beyond my last breath to my eternal destiny. It's good to have my life in His hands.

Some locals told me that Dale's was a great place to eat so down the steps and off to Dale's I went to grab some lunch.

The place was busy but I found a spot to sit. The food was like mom's kitchen and yes, mom is a great cook. The portions were generous with fresh bottomless coffee. The local people were very friendly and helpful in guiding me to eating places and places of interest as I wondered around the streets.

After browsing more places downtown, I headed back up the south slope to the house. Brian could tell I was in a better mood so he asked," How about us going fishing tomorrow? " We had packed some poles just in case we had some time on this trip.

"Okay, sounds like fun. I'm sure Tim knows some good fishing spots."

I was glad we were back on speaking terms again. I'm sure Tim and Gayle were also glad to see the atmosphere had cleared. No more storm clouds tonight. At supper Tim told us about some place called Cold Brook to try our luck at fishing. At least we would be doing something together.

After a good night's sleep we were off to the fishing hole. Winding around hills and valleys we found the place. Setting up our rigs and casting in our lines we settled down to just wait for a bite.

I sensed that Brian had something on his mind. At first it was just small talk as we took in the scenery and listened to the birds. Finally, I felt that he was going to get to the point.

With a deep breath Brian opened up, "Dad?"

"Yes, Brian."

"Do you remember why I called it quits on the trail?"

"Sure, because you were cold and tired"

"No, it was because I did not want to spend another night in that stupid tent!"

"Okay, what's your point?"

"Dad, what would you think of a plan B?"

"Okay, you got my attention. Let's hear it."

"What if we reserved a room at the end of each day? It's the tail end of tourist season so we have a better chance to get a place. Think about a nice soft warm bed waiting for us at the end of the day."

"You know Brian that just might work. First we could get dropped off at Rochford by Gayle before she goes to work, and then the next night's stop would be Hill City. The next day we stop in Pringle. All we need is a place to stay at Hill City and Pringle because Edgemont is the finish line."

"You know, Dad, if we quit fishing now we won't have to clean any."

"Sounds good, let's see if we can find some lodging in Hill City and Pringle."

With that we picked up our fishing gear and went back to town. We started looking for lodging pamphlets. The thought of still walking the Mickelson Trail got me excited again. The only thing that could stop us was not finding places to stay.

After a few phone calls, we found a number of places in Hill City but no place in Pringle. Maybe Tim and Gayle might know of some places in Pringle and Hill City. I knew we would be imposing on them to drop us off at Rochford again but without their help we would be sunk.

There were some small cabins on the edge of Hill City that looked perfect to us. They had a kitchenette, restroom, and a shower. I thought I'd better call and see if they had a vacancy. We could always cancel if it didn't work out. With a deep breath I dialed the number. A friendly voice answered and informed me that they did have a cabin vacancy, so I booked it.

"Hey Brian, the cabin at Hill City is a go". He gave me a big thumb up. Now, what about Pringle?

As Tim and Gayle got home from work they could see we were excited about something.

Brian busted out with, "Guess what? We have a plan B for the Mickelson Trail!"

At the supper table we began to work on the details of the plan. Tim and Gayle agreed to drop us off at Rochford so that hurdle was cleared. I explained that we had a place we could stay at Hill City but Pringle was a problem.

Gayle said "That one's easy; Pringle isn't that far from here. We can pick you up and drop you back off on the trail in the morning."

"Let me make it easier for you, I piped in. Pringle to Edgemont is the home stretch. We can drive ourselves back to Pringle in the morning and leave the vehicle there. After we complete the trail, you come get us at Edgemont, and then we can pick-up our vehicle in Pringle, on the way back to Hot Springs".

The chatter around the table was as lively as the day we first came. Now that we had fine- tuned plan B, we went to our rooms to repack. The load will be lighter because we won't have to drag along tents and camping gear. Tomorrow morning we'll hit the trail again!

CHAPTER THIRTEEN

The ring of an alarm clock can be irritating, but that day it meant a second chance. We had to get an early start so Gayle could get back in time for work. Going back to Rochford felt totally different than the defeated feeling we had when we left. It wasn't every day we got a redo.

We arrived just before sunrise. After Gayle dropped us off, it was Brian and I and the trail once again. A cold shiver went down my back as I looked at the place that was our last campsite. We could have died there. That was a night we'll never forget. We were survivors, now it's time to take on the world.

With each step down the trail we put that awful tent site further behind us. We didn't need those cheap tents or camping gear. Our backpacks were lighter. The rhythmic crunch of each stride pushed us forward like the beat of a song. Each step was progressively making our spirits soar.

Around the next bend we saw something that would be transfixed in my mind for the rest of my life. We froze in awe of what stood before us. There was a great archway with a brilliant light shining through. This tunnel looked like we were about to walk through the gates of Heaven and into God's glory. We couldn't see beyond the light but we knew we wouldn't be disappointed. Emotional tears ran down my cheeks. It felt as though if we proceeded through there would be no return. This reminded me of Patricia's dream. I wonder if this was something like what she saw as she went to her final home.

"You know Brian; this feels like a sacred place. We are here at the right place, the right season, in the right weather, at the right time. Maybe God has a message for us?"

"Dad, how can a person put words to what we are looking at?"

With a deep breath we moved forward. Passing through the tunnel, the warmth of the sunlight compelled us forward. As we exited the other side, the light danced with the shadows over the valleys below. I felt like I could stretch forth my arms and fly with the eagles and Heavenly Hosts. A tap on my shoulder brought me back down to earth.

"Dad, I know this is beautiful, but we have a lot of ground to cover."

Each person that walks this trail will never forget the experience. Moving forward we were greeted by another tunnel. Each one had its own character and opened us to even more beauty. There were four tunnels in all. Each one had to be big enough for a train to go through. I can't imagine the hard work it must have been to carve out all that rock by hand with picks and shovels. There had to have been risk to this project. For all I know there could have been loss of life to accomplish such a task.

The pathway leveled off for a while around Mystic Road. We were surrounded by hardwood trees like Aspen, Birch, and Elms. I'll bet this place is a burst of color in the fall.

A large feather caught my eye along the side of the road. It was from a wild turkey. I picked it up and stuck in my cap. This will be my lucky feather. Native Americans tell me that if an eagle gives up a feather that means God had heard their prayers. I don't know what a turkey feather means except that it will be my good luck feather. If I saw a buzzard feather, I wouldn't pick it up. To me, they are a sign of death. No thank you, no buzzard feathers for me! Those birds won't be picking on my bones anytime soon.

As we pushed forward, the trail became hills and pine trees again. The sun was working its way to the western sky. We were winding our way around another bend when we heard a welcome sound of a train whistle. The echoes of that old steam engine that came down the valleys made us stop and listen. You just don't hear that sound much anymore. It's a blast from the past. To me, a steam whistle sounds like a fine tuned instrument. It is pure music to my ears.

"Brian, do you know what that is?"

"It sounds like a train."

"It not just any train. It's the 1880 train from Hill City. Our destination might be just around the next bend." With that thought we picked up the pace.

The 1880 Train ran from Hill City to Keystone and back. The trip took about an hour each way, plus a 15 minute stop in Keystone. Thousands of

tourists took the ride each year. There just aren't
as many steam engines as there were in times past.

That whistle triggered a fond memory of years past when Christy
and Brian were little. Patricia and I took them on this train trip.
I'm so glad we did. It's easy to say we'll do it someday, but we
did it and the whole family had a lifetime of precious memories.

The sound of the whistle must have carried for miles through
the hills, because we just kept going around bends and over hills
for an hour or so.

As we crested a hill, there it was, nestled in the valley. Side
by side we ambled down the hill to the night's destiny, Hill City.

Suddenly, I heard something behind us. I looked back just
in time to see a bicycle bearing down on us at full speed. In a
split second I reacted by pushing Brian off the path and jump-
ing back. The biker flew by and didn't even look back to see if
we were okay.

"Brian, you Okay? What an idiot."

"No, Dad I think I sprained my ankle."

In a flash we went from triumph to tragedy. My face burned.
I clinched my teeth. My whole body began to shake. If I could
just get ahold of that pea brain!

Most people were thoughtful, they would let us know they
were coming up behind us, and then pass us slowly. That jerk
thought this trail was his race track. I wonder if he thought it
was funny to see us scatter. For a while my thoughts of what to
do to that guy was not too pleasant, but I had to shake it off and
cool down. I needed to concentrate on Brian's needs.

He hobbled over to me and I supported his injured side. We slowly descended the hill into town. I could almost feel each painful step he took as we worked our way through town and to the Pine Rest Cabins.

After getting the key I got Brian on to a nice soft bed and elevated his injured foot. Then I was off to a convenience store for some crushed ice and something for us to eat.

The cabin was a nice clean place with a couple beds, shower, AC, and a kitchenette. If it weren't for worrying about Brian, I would have enjoyed kicking back and relaxing.

Through the night we kept icing that elevated ankle. Moans in the night told me that once again we would be calling Gayle to come get us in the morning.

This journey felt cursed. Defeat settled in again. In a feeble attempt I prayed, "Lord, why can't you just heal his ankle?" With a heavy heart, I finally drifted off to sleep.

CHAPTER FOURTEEN

My trusty biological clock woke me before sunrise even though I didn't get a full night's sleep. There was a pit in my stomach; unforeseen things just keep knocking us down on this trail. I hated the thought of calling Gayle again to come get us. I sat at the little kitchen table thinking of what we should do. If we stayed in Hill City all day, Gayle would not have to pick us up until after work. Maybe I could go into town and get Brian a walking cane. My thoughts were interrupted by a stirring from Brian's bed. He sat up and stretched.

Looking over his way I just had to ask, "So how are you feeling this morning?"

"Surprisingly, not bad, he replied, if I stand up and put some weight on this foot that will tell us how bad it is."

"Wait, Brian," I yelled as I got up from my chair.

I ran over to him in case he crumpled to the floor in pain. With a step down on the sore ankle, Brian replied, "There's no sharp pain, it's just a little stiff. Maybe if I walk around it'll loosen up."

As he carefully walked around the room, I kept a close eye on him.

"Dad, I think we can still do this."

"Really, are you just trying to push past the pain to prove you're not a quitter?'

"Let's go get some breakfast, and see if my ankle holds up. That will determine our next move."

We grabbed our belongings and did a last walk around to make sure nothing got left behind. Then it was off to the office to drop off the keys. There we saw a coffee pot and continental breakfast. To me, a good day starts with a good cup of coffee.

"Oh yes, coffee, let me have this moment."

"Dad, you're so predictable."

Sitting down to a table we began to make plans. If we couldn't get far we would just stay in Hill City until Tim and Gayle got off work. Then they could come get us. There was plenty to see and do right here.

This leg of the walk would take us through two towns: Custer and Pringle. We would arrive in Custer around noon and Pringle at the end of the day. If we made it to Custer, we would see how Brian's ankle was holding out. No matter what, Tim and Gayle will be coming to get us. It would be nice if we could make it all the way to Pringle, but I'll be watching my walking partner closely.

Back on the Mickelson Trail, we started out slowly. I noticed a slight limp. This could go either way. Brian could walk it off or things could get worse. I said a silent pray as we gently moved along.

"Brian, what do you think? How do you feel?"

"Like I said earlier, there's no sharp pain-- just stiffness, so far so good."

A few miles down the road, we could hear water roaring beyond a knoll off to the side of the path. We just had to check it out. Cresting the small hill we were greeted by the smell of a fresh mountain stream. There was two little water falls about 50 feet apart. Pine trees hung over the rocky banks making this place a little paradise. If I lived in the area, I'd come here often. What a place to destress. The fresh air, the sounds of the water, and the beauty made this place really special. I broke out my point and shoot camera and got a number of pictures. If they come out as good as this looked, I might do an oil painting of this place.

Back on the trail, every now and then we would come across a wild raspberry patch. Boy, what a treat. Sometimes we walked out into open meadows. Once we saw a family in a small stream panning for gold. I waved and yelled good luck as we passed by.

Around noon we came to Custer. Finding a nice family restaurant, we settled in for a good meal. It was time to reassess the ankle.

"Well Brian, what do you think? I noticed you're not limping as much."

"Yeah, I think it's going to be alright."

"The stretch between here and Pringle is going to be a pretty long jaunt. Are you sure?"

"Dad, I'm good as gold."

After that response, I sent up a silent thank you prayer.

"OK, then its Pringle or bust. Sorry Brian, poor choice of words."

Our chuckles were interrupted by a ring on my cell phone. The hills have a lot of dead zones but in Custer the signal came through.

"Jim! Are you guys alright?" Do you know how hard it is to get ahold of you?"

"Yes Mom, There are a lot of dead zones in the hills; today you just happened to catch us in Custer."

After getting Mom up to speed on the highlights of the trip and letting her know we were still alive, it was time to get back on the road. With a full stomach, we headed out again.

A short ways past Custer, there was a doe and her twin fawns just 30 feet off the side of the path. She had no fear. She was as curious of us as we were of her. I even got to stop and get a picture. After that she slowly turned and walked away with her fawns following right behind. It was as if she said "Okay, you got your picture now, it's time for us to go."

The landscape leveled off for a few miles and the road was as straight as an arrow. There were clusters of rock formations on each side, with grasslands and meadows surrounding them. The scenery was always changing as we hiked the Mickelson Trail.

We noticed that the temperature was getting hotter. To think a few days back we were freezing to death, it was hard to believe that a few days down the road, and we would be melting in the heat. It was a good thing the trail heads were only about ten miles apart. As we came to one of them, we refilled our water bottles and got out some headbands that had little beads in them that expanded and stayed cool as we ran cold water over them. Wrapping them around our heads cooled us off. It was always good to be prepared for everything. After a stop at the outhouse, it was onward and forward.

We were making good time that day. As we headed into another cluster of trees something made me freeze.

"Brian, stop!" I commanded in a low quiet voice.

"What's the matter?" he whispered back.

I pointed downward as I muttered "Look at the ground just ahead of us. There, do you see it?"

It was a fresh set of large cat tracks. I felt the hair on the back of my neck stand up. There could be a mountain lion perched up in a tree watching our every move with its icy stare.

I reached to my side to see if my pepper spray was still in place. Okay good, I'm all set. Next we went over what to do if we encountered one. My fight and flight instinct was about to kick in. But I knew the outcome could have been devastating. After I pulled myself together, we slowly walked forward through the trees. Every once in a while I'd look back to see if we were being followed. When we came out the other side of the woods, I felt better.

"See, that cat was probably more afraid of us then we were of it," Brian piped up with a smirk.

"Maybe if there was only one of us, the outcome might have been different," I responded.

Farther down the road, we came across a pile of bones. I pointed them out to Brian.

"Not everyone got out alive," I chanted. It was probably deer bones, but I made my point.

Brian chuckled.

I recognized a set of buildings close to Pringle. The shack was nestled on the top of a small rocky ledge. I had done a couple of oil paintings of it from a couple of different angles a few years back.

Just ahead was our day's destination, Pringle. I sent another prayer God's way thanking Him for Brian's ankle recovery. We covered a little over 25 miles that day and worked up a pretty good appetite.

The main business in town was the Hitchrail Bar and Restaurant. This place has a lot of unusual features, like deer antlers for door pulls. There are many elk head mounts as well as mounts of deer and other animals. A lot of knotty pine graced its walls. I really liked this game lodge atmosphere. Our burgers were thick and juicy, putting other burger joints to shame. Tim and Gayle told me this place is known for its homemade kettle chips so we just had to try them. A juicy burger and those chips just knocked it out of the park.

"You know what, Brian? This turned out to be a pretty good day."

"It started out kind of shaky, but you bet, it did turn out real good."

The door opened and Tim and Gayle came in.

I turned, "Hi guys, perfect timing, did you eat yet?"

They ordered some food and kettle chips and we told them the ups and downs of the last couple days. Tonight we planned to hit the hay early. Of the legs of the trail, tomorrow would be the longest.

Back in Hot Springs, it sure felt good to lie down in a nice soft bed after a long day. We sat our alarms to get going early.

The plan was to drive ourselves back to Pringle and leave the vehicle there till we came back for it in the evening.

Tomorrow, we would need to pick up something to eat before hitting the trail, because there would be no places between Pringle and Edgemont to eat. The fact that the last leg would be the longest and most isolated made me a little nervous, but we could not stop now.

CHAPTER FIFTEEN

Even in my sleep I knew that morning was the big day! My eyes popped wide open early, well before sunrise. That day it was like rounding 3rd base and heading for home plate. That day we would be hiking more miles than any other day on the trail. It stood to reason that the longer the trail, the longer the risk. Will we make it before dark? There were so many things going through my head. Nothing was going to stop us, even if we had to drag our bodies across the finish line.

After grabbing our back packs and supplies, Brian and I headed to the first convenience store that was open. We found some trail mix and fruit to get us through the day, and then I followed my nose to my favorite drink. Oh yes, Coffee! If ever I needed a good fresh start, that tall warm cup was it.

We saw a slight tinge of light shown down on Pringle, as we pulled into town and parked by the Mickelson Trail.

"Well Brian, This is it. We need to pace ourselves. If we go too fast we could burn out, but we must go fast enough to get to Edgemont before the sun goes down."

"After all we been through, we got this, Dad," he replied with great confidence.

Our adrenaline ran high when we set foot on the trail. As we pushed forward, the only sound was the crunch under our feet. This trail reminded me of a wild horse. It felt untamed and unpredictable, yet with each step it was becoming an old friend.

It usually took about a mile for us to get in sync. Crunch, crunch, crunch, crunch, the rhythm was like the beat of a catchy song. I noticed Brian was spending less time on his MP3 player and more time soaking in the surroundings of nature.

To the left of us, an old set of buildings came into sight. I found it quite gratifying that there were historic markers with details about what was before us. This was the remains of an old lime stone plant. The Black Hills Lime Company provided lime by rail to places around the hills. It is a key component in concrete. I snapped a number of pictures of the sight and sign to study later, but for now it was time to push forward.

The landscape around us was changing. It became rolling hills and flat prairie. What was once granite became red dirt and shale. The pine trees became hardwoods and sage brush. It was funny how much change you can see in one trail.

Up ahead I saw something that looked suspicious. We knew that most vehicles were restricted from the trail but there was a pickup truck right in front of us. The land around us was isolated. If these guys ahead of us were bad news, there would be no one around to help us. The thought of being at the wrong place at the wrong time came to mind. If someone disposed of a body in a shallow grave would anyone find it out here?

"Brian, does that look a little suspicious to you?"

"Yeah, it's possible that they could be trouble, let's proceed with caution."

I knew my mind liked to hype up the imagination, but what if these guys were up to no good? I also knew that they saw us. Once again, I checked to see if my pepper spray was in place. The element of surprise could swing in our favor should a struggle occur.

Both Brian and I had been pushed into fights in the past. We tried to avoid fights at all costs because we had a trait that was not pleasant. Both of us tend to go into a trance that made us feel no pain and someone had to stop us or we could kill the poor guy. There was no one out here to stop us. My imagination does like to go wild.

As we got closer, I saw they were in uniform. The pickup was a government vehicle. They were park rangers, the good guys, inspecting and maintaining the trail. We both breathed a deep sigh of relief. Brian and I didn't want to hurt anyone. I just couldn't pass by without thanking them for the great job caring for the trail. It was clean and well maintained all the way. We shared how we started walking from Deadwood and now we're on the home stretch.

One of the rangers responded, "We get a lot of bikers on the trail, but not many that walk the whole thing. Just a minute, we have something for you."

He reached into the backseat of the pick-up and pulled out a small Mickelson Trail marker.

"This one has some scratches on it. If we find one with some damage, we have to replace it."

"Wow," I responded, "this will be our trophy plate. We will treasure this for a lifetime, thank you."

Placing it into my backpack, it was time to move on. Cresting a rolling hill, we could see that the path was as straight as an arrow getting smaller and smaller till it reached a vanishing point on the far horizon. A bit of panic stirred up inside of me. I knew we still had a long way to go. Edgemont was beyond that vanishing point. We needed to pick up the pace a little.

Lunch was on the run. We munched on our trail mix and fruit on the move. When we finished eating, the bags went back into our backpacks until we came to a trash can. It was important to us to leave the trail as clean as we found it.

For a while, we were on automatic pilot lost in our own thoughts. The crunch, crunch, crunch of our steps was hypnotizing. In time, we came to a trail head station. Another park ranger was tidying up the rest area. This pleasant young ranger lady came to meet us.

"Are you guys hiking the whole trail?" she asked.

"Well yes, we are." I piped up.

She responded, "I feel that deserves some recognition. Let me give you a pamphlet with an address you can write to get a certificate for your achievement."

Brian and I thanked her as I placed it in my backpack with our little trail marker. This felt like a video game where you got points as you proceeded. After a drink and filling up our water bottles, we were off again.

The trail began to wind around some rolling hills. Small washouts appeared between them with some cotton wood trees along their banks. We saw another cement mileage marker just ahead.

"Hey Brian, check this out! It's the ten mile marker; from this point forward it will be our countdown to the finish line. Do you realize we have walked about a 100 miles?"

"Yeah, that's big, now just ten miles to go. Let's do this!"

We took each other's picture by the marker before moving on.

Soon some big red shale gorges with pine trees filled the landscape. The Mickelson Trail was just full of surprises. At the top of a hill we saw the prairie below, but better yet, we saw the Celestial City like in Pilgrims Progress. At least it felt like it. A flood of emotion came over us. We were almost there.

One thing haunted me; the path didn't go straight to Edgemont. It swung off to the right and came back to the town from the side. That added more distance to the home stretch.

As we descended out of the hills onto the prairie, the sun was also descending towards the western horizon. Urgency came over us. We had to get to the finish line before dark. The flatland made the miles seem longer.

When the town was to our side, we crossed the train tracks. The path turned and headed into Edgemont parallel to the railroad. The trail markers read 5-4-3-2. This countdown was almost over. With the sun setting, my adrenalin kicked in again. I began to jog. Brian didn't feel that was necessary. He yelled something at me that I didn't quite understand, but I don't think it was, "Go Dad go." About that time, Tim and Gayle pulled up near us on the side road. "We'll see you at the finish," Tim yelled as they drove by.

Turning into town, the gravel trail became asphalt streets. Little signs let us know we were still on course. I backed off my pace so Brian could catch up. For some reason I didn't think he was happy with me, but I got his point. It wasn't a race and we started together so we should finish together.

Looking ahead, I saw our last obstacle. "Oh no, not now," I thought as we got closer. There sat Tim and Gayle at a railroad crossing waiting for a stopped train to move. We'd walked over a 100 miles without being blocked by a train until now. There was only a quarter mile to go to the end. I felt like walking up and kicking the train. Some things were just out of our control. Frustration built up within. To be this close to the finish line and have to wait, my patience was worn thin. The light was disappearing quickly. All I could do was pace back and forth.

Finally, a banging of railroad cars signaled that the train was about to move. With a slow start, the cars moved by. There were box cars, coal cars, flat cars, and tankers. Then there were more box cars, coal cars, flat cars, and tankers. Faster and faster they moved, then after what seemed an eternity, the end car came into sight as the last of the twilight disappeared. At last we had the street lights to guide us onward.

We crossed the tracks, and turned onto the main street that headed into the city park. At the other end of the park we could see the finish line. A large crowd of Tim and Gayle clapped and cheered us on. With a flood of emotions we reached the end of the Mickelson Trail.

After 109 miles of triumphs and tragedies, highs and lows, we finally made it! With hugs from the crowd, (Tim and Gayle), and tears of accomplishment, it was picture time. Flash pictures were taken beside the trail marker to prove our accomplishment.

It was time to go eat at the café on the main drag of Edgemont. This occasion called for a nice steak. The meal was great. It tasted like victory.

Before moving on I had to call Christy and Mom to let them know we made it.

On the ride back to Pringle to pick up our vehicle, we shared all the ups and downs of the day's journey. Brian and I were tired but content. To think, we almost gave up a couple of times. Oh, to persevere, we did it! I remember thinking I'm not a loser after all.

After picking up our vehicle, the drive to Hot Springs was quiet. Brian was resting and I was replaying the whole trip in my mind. As I settled into bed that night I knew that my biological clock didn't need to get me up early the next morning. It was mission accomplished.

CHAPTER SIXTEEN

Tim and Gayle's house was quiet when I woke up. Brian was still snoring away. Tim and Gayle were off to work already. We said our good- byes last night. It was time to head home. I thought of Rufus and Rosey, our dogs. I'm sure they missed us. To sleep in our own beds sounded so good. Yes, it was time for these happy wanderers to return to their roost. I could hear Brian starting to stir in the other room. It didn't take him long to be up and about. We packed up our gear, did a walk through to see if we forgot anything, and then we were on our way home.

Before leaving town, we grabbed a bite to eat and enjoyed some nice warm coffee. I just can't imagine what life would be like without coffee. Like an old friend, it's been there for me.

The plan was to make it a simple travel day. We had enough sightseeing for this trip. It was time to just get home. From Hot Springs to Huron takes about six hours. Maybe we'll stop in Wall for a buffalo burger and a cup of their world famous five-cent coffee,

"Hey, Brian, Did you know there were more people who climbed Mount Everest than did what we just did? Walking the Mickelson Trail was a big deal."

"You bet! It was harder than I thought it would be, but we did it. The thing is we persevered, we didn't give up."

"I got a great idea, Brian, what if we walked from the east border of South Dakota to the west border?"

"HELL NO, Dad, NO MORE HAIR BRAINED IDEAS!"

"I was just teasing you."

"That wasn't funny, that was enough walking for a lifetime."

But after that comment, we looked each other in the eye and started laughing.

Brian was driving and the radio was playing songs on an oldies station. Somewhere along the way, I drifted off to sleep. A strange wailing sound woke me up. What on earth? The sound was coming from me! I was being ambushed in my sleep by my deep painful emotions. What brought that on? Was it an old song on the radio? It caught me totally off guard.

"Dad, Dad? Are you okay?"

I couldn't answer because I was sobbing uncontrollably. It was hard to catch my breath. Eight months had gone by since Patricia passed on, but my grief was still raw. I don't think Brian had ever seen me breakdown like that.

When I could finally speak, I responded, "Wow where did that come from? I wasn't prepared for that! I'll be fine."

We didn't go into how we felt too much. Maybe it would have been better if we had. Maybe seeing me break down might have helped Brian understand how much I loved his mother. At that time it still was a little awkward to talk about things.

When I brought that deep down pain within me to the surface, something strange happened. The pain became warm tears that ran down my face. It felt cleansing. Somehow I felt a little better. After that, tears came easier for me. The flood gate was opening. The healing process was underway.

I grew up believing men don't cry, that's a lie, even Jesus wept. To be tough, only makes us hold it in and that can hurt us down the road.

After a few hours, Brian pulled into the city of Wall. I pulled myself together in time for buffalo burgers and five-cent coffee. It felt good to get the kinks out before getting back to the highway to head home. Our bellies were full so we were ready to hit the road again.

It was my turn to drive. Heading east, the land leveled off into slightly rolling hills and flat prairie. Brian reclined his seat and took a nap.

When I'm behind the driver's seat, I did a lot of thinking. I've been told I am analytical. I analyze things constantly. This time my focus was on the George S. Mickelson Trail.

What blessings did I get walking the trail?

Was the effort worth it?

Accomplishments

When I first lost Patricia, I felt like my life was over also, all that was left was sitting back in an easy chair watching TV and waiting for my time to die. The planning of the trip and the hike itself helped give me life again. I had to try. I made a promise to Patricia. Push forward, that's what I had to do. Buzzards don't circle over a moving body. I'm not dead yet.

Brian and I did this together. We took problems and made them into challenges, and then we conquered them. The two of us were survivors. With a smile I looked over at Brian as we slept. I guess we made a pretty good team.

Treasured Memories

There were many things on the trail I will remember, but two places stood out. The tunnel with the light shining through was like a glimpse of the gates of Heaven. Brian and I were at the right place at the right time.

That tranquil place by Hill City with the two waterfalls was so peaceful. I may not get to see it again but I can always go there in my thoughts. The smell of the fresh spring water, the sound of the rushing stream, and the beauty that surrounded us will be in my mind for a lifetime.

On those dark days of depression, I can sit back, take a deep breath, and go to those beautiful places in my mind.

What I learned on the trail

If something doesn't work out. Don't give up. Look for a plan B. When we stayed overnight at Hill City, it made the completion of the hike possible.

I wished I would have researched what to expect at the higher altitudes. Who knew that it could get that cold in August at night? That was an amateur's mistake.

Looking ahead, I could tell we were almost home. It's time for Brian to wake up.

"Hey Brian, I see Huron just ahead of us."

"Ummu, that's nice Dad. Wake me when we're at the front door."

"Come on, you can't sleep your life away."

"Maybe not, but I'd like to give it a try."

"BRIAN, WAKE UP!"

Okay, okay, I'm awake.

It was good to be back in Huron. I pulled up into the driveway and headed to the door. I could hear the pounding of little paws from within the house. It sounded like a stampede. What an enthusiastic welcome we received! I could tell Rufus and Rosey were well taken care of. Duane always has had a caring heart for people and animals. It sure felt good to be home.

CHAPTER SEVENTEEN

It felt so good to wake up in my own bed. Dorothy from *The Wizard of OZ*, said it right, there's no place like home. If I could lay here till noon that would be nice, but my back would start to stiffen up and then I'd hurt for the rest of the day. Besides, my four legged friends knew I was awake and they wouldn't leave me alone until I took them out.

As I got up, the dogs danced around the floor impatiently. I don't know why they call dog owners masters. It seems like we are the ones serving them.

I didn't need to worry about getting Brian up; he earned some extra sleep. I didn't want him to wake up crabby so I decided to let him sleep in. He's not much of a morning person and I'm sure the extra rest helped.

As the days passed by, I got the prints of the photos I took along the trail. I spread them out on the table in order, and then I picked out the best ones to put into a DVD. I thought it would be nice to show to friends and family.

One day I got a manila envelope from the park service. I eagerly opened it and there in my hands were two signed and certified certificates verifying what we accomplished on the George Mickelson Trail.

Brian walked into the room and asked "Is that the mail?"

"It sure is. Bet you can't guess what we got?"

"Let's see, a year's supply of candy bars."

"Nope, not even close."

"Is it an invitation to a national talk show?"

"Yeah, that would really be something we could only dream. I'm sorry no. But we did get our certified certificates from the parks department. Here is yours."

Brian studied it over and responded, "Yup looks official." Then he took his downstairs.

I took mine and put it with the little trail marker that a park ranger gave us, then I placed it in a safe place. After that I sat down to reflect on the last few weeks.

As I sat there with my coffee in hand, my thoughts were interrupted by the clicking of little toe nails on the linoleum. First Rufus came up to me, wanting some attention. He loved it when I'd scratch him behind the ears. Then Rosey came up as if to say. Why should Rufus get all the attention?

While I was petting my fury friends, my mind went back to the journey of grief. There are so many types of grief.

We should never take lightly the pain of loss, even the loss of a pet. They can leave a big impact on our lives. I have mourned for some real special dogs. Each one I cared about deeply.

Rufus and Rosey helped me stay in shape. We all enjoyed our daily walks. It would have been too easy to just sit back in my recliner, watch TV, and get back into my old rut. Not only would my physical condition have gone downhill, but my emotional state would have declined also.

After the big hike was over, I needed more goals. They didn't need to be as big as the trail, but it was important that I had something to look forward to, something to reach for.

Of all the photos I took on the Mickelson Trail, one stood out. It was that tranquil place by Hill City. My mind went back to the sound of the waterfalls, the smell by the fresh spring fed stream, and the beauty of the landscape.

I enlarged the photo to an 8 by 10. Then I got a 16 by 20 canvas and prepared it for an oil painting. If that photo could talk, it would have screamed paint me.

It was good that I had some projects; the worst thing I could have done was to have stayed at home and avoided people. If I had withdrawn into myself, it would have slowly killed me. I'm a social person. My favorite thing is engaging in conversation. You might say the gift of gab. On Sundays I can be one of the last people out of the church building. The insight of others captivates me. For me to have withdrawn, I would have withered on the vine.

Getting back with the photo club and writers group helped fill some of the void of engagement with others, but it was the reuniting with the grief support group that helped me the most.

As time went by, I was asked if I would be a facilitator (a group leader). I told them I needed some time to think it over.

Weighing the pros and cons, I knew I would have to share my painful journey with others. Yet maybe this was a way to find purpose in my loss. It's true I can relate to other people's pain. Other people helped me, so why not? The thought of walking along side someone else in that dark journey made sense to me. No one was to walk it alone. With training and encouragement, I found myself helping others in a group session.

One thing I had to learn was to be a better listener. I had to keep reminding myself that God gave me two ears but only one mouth so I should listen twice as much as speak. To listen means to give them my undivided attention. I shouldn't be thinking of what I'm going to say next.

When I think about journeys, I realized that I'd always be on some kind of journey. Some I choose and some choose me. Like the journey of grief, those are the ones that are hard to prepare for. It's strange to think we can travel on more than one journey at a time like Brian and I did as we walked the Mickelson Trail. Grief's journey came with us.

The journey of grief can be like that. It's hard just to move forward, with the help of faith, family, friends, and a grief support group; it's possible to move forward.

It was glorious to reach the finish line on the trail, but the journey of grief still continued. The only way I could show that progress, was to kick the timeline down the road a few years.

It took a while to realize my loss wasn't just about me. Others felt the sting of grief also. For the longest time I really didn't reach out to Christy and Brian. I regretted that.

Christy was a little more open to getting help. She attended a grief support group in Sioux Falls where her husband, Jonathan, and family live. She once told me the day after she gave birth to Kaleb, her first born, that the next day she heard her mother had stage four cancer. During one of the greatest joys in life, the news squashed some of that joy. She wandered if Kaleb would ever get to know his grandmother. Ultimately, Patricia got to read a story book to him on his second birthday.

Brian moved to Sioux Falls for more job opportunities. His journey of grief was a real struggle. He was in a dark place for quite awhile. Brian would rather hold in those emotions. He had a hard time talking about those taboo subjects. One day he called me and I could tell he was stressed out.

"Dad, can we talk?"

I braced myself for bad news. "Okay, Brian I'm all ears."

"I've been holding in all this pain and sorrow for so long. Do you have time to listen?"

"Of course, take all the time you need."

Inside I was dancing with joy. Brian was finally opening up! We must have talked for two hours. Much of the past of his mother's death was a blur to me. I got to hear some of the pieces of the puzzle I didn't remember about that horrible night. Like where was Brian that night?" He and I took turns helping Patricia. We bought a baby monitor so if she had a need, we could be right there. That night Brian was working on a project out in the garage. I sat by Patricia's bedside as she took her last breath. To honor her wishes, I did not try to resuscitate. Instead, I kissed her on the forehead and sang our favorite hymn, *In the Garden,* as a final send-off. Then I called hospice and they did what needed to be done.

I remember the coroner checking her pulse and reading off the time of death. Than they zipped her up in a body bag and wheeled her out. I'll never forget them zipping that bag over her face. I played that scene over and over in my mind. After that it was just me and the hospice lady. I couldn't remember anything else. What I didn't know was that Brian was listening to the whole thing on the monitor and couldn't bring himself to come in the house. Poor Brian, he heard me saying good-bye. He also heard me sing the send-off song. Then he heard the coroner read off the time of death. Brian always went to his mother for comfort, but the comforter was gone. As for me, I was in shock and void of emotion, so I was no help to anyone. I could feel the pain as he shared all this. Tears streamed down my face as he poured out his heart.

After that conversation I felt that was the turning point of Brian's healing process. We are walking side by side now on the grief journey, both moving forward. There is no subject that's off the table anymore. As father and son we are the closest we've ever been.

So what's it like farther down the road of grief? I know we all grieve differently. If we work on getting through it, and not run from it, our odds are better that we get past the hardest part of grief. This stage of my grief, the pain isn't near as sharp. I still miss her but I come to terms with things. My desire is to see her again in Glory. I remember special things about her. Some things make me smile and other things make me chuckle. Like when one morning she asked me, "Why does morning always have to come so early?" That will stay with me for the rest of my life.

I tell those that think their pain will last forever, if they work through their grief, someday they will smile again and some day they can laugh again without feeling guilty. Some day they can even enjoy life again. Right now they are looking at life through pain. Hang in there. Life gets better. They just have to do the leg work.

When I was in the U.S Navy, I weathered many a storm. There was only one way for a vessel to survive huge storms. Here is a poem I wrote about my experiences at sea.

A Ship in the Storm

If a ship tries to out run a storm. It can be over
taken and pulled down.

If a ship tries to go to the side of a storm, the
waves can side-swipe it and overturn it belly-up.

But if a ship faces a storm head-on, even though
the waves hit, the ship cuts though

and comes out the other side safely.

So if we run from our problems, they will catch
up to us.

If we try to sidestep our problems, they can
turn our world upside down. But if we face our
problems,

We see them coming and with the Lord's help,

We work our way through them,

And come out the other side victorious.

James A W Schmidt

Made in the USA
Middletown, DE
26 September 2021